For Mum and Dad - Adam

A TEMPLAR BOOK

First published in the UK in hardback in 2005 by Templar Publishing,
This softback edition published in 2005 by Templar Publishing,
an imprint of The Templar Company Limited,
The Granary, North Street, Dorking, Surrey, RH4 1DN, UK
www.templarco.co.uk

10 9 8 7 6 5 4 3 2

The illustrations in this book
were rendered in brush, ink and watercolour.

ISBN 978-1-84011-196-5

Printed in Hong Kong

wap
wap
wap

A tale of consequences by Adam Stower, called...

huff, puff, huff, puff, huff, pu

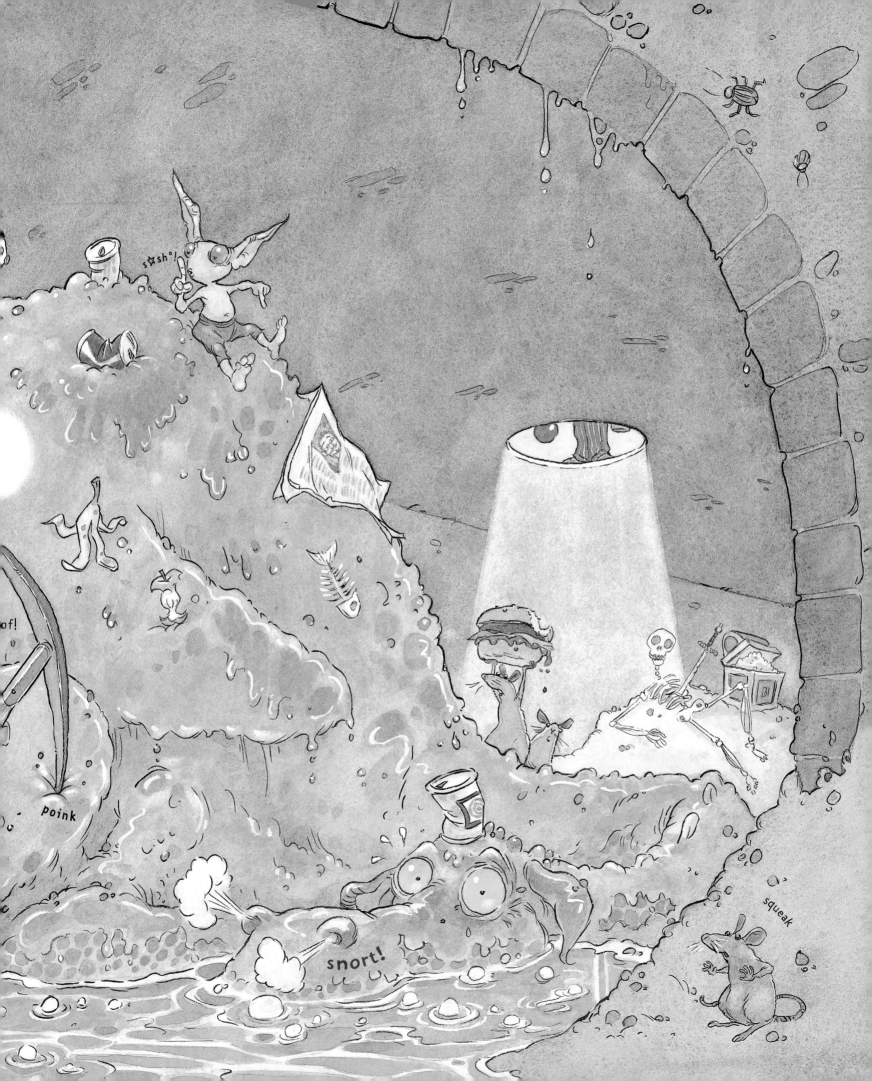

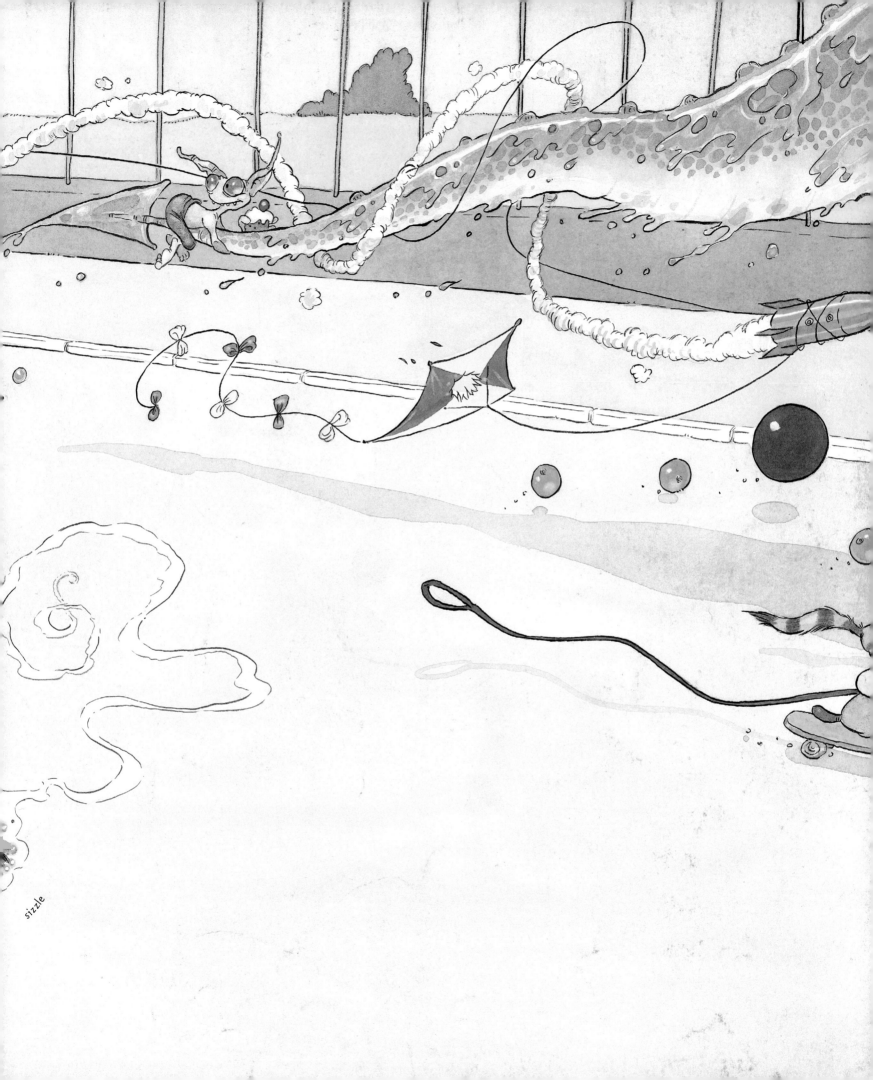

sizzle